ESCAPE FROM PLANET ALCATRAZ

PRISONERS OF THE POISON SEA

Raintree is an imprint of Capstone Global Library Limited, a company incorporated in England and Wales having its registered office at 264 Banbury Road, Oxford, OX2 7DY – Registered company number: 6695582

www.raintree.co.uk
myorders@raintree.co.uk

Edited by Aaron J Sautter
Designed by Kay Fraser
Original illustrations © Capstone Global Library Limited 2020
Production by Katy LaVigne
Originated by Capstone Global Library Ltd
Printed and bound in India

ISBN: 978 1 4747 8490 0 (paperback)

British Library Cataloguing in Publication Data
A full catalogue record for this book is available from the British Library.

Acknowledgements
Design elements: Shutterstock: Agustina Camilion, A-Star, Dima Zel, Draw_Wing_Zen, Hybrid_Graphics, Metallic Citizen

TALK ABOUT IT

1. Zak and Erro start the story lost in a freezing sandstorm. Can you think of any ways the boys could have better protected themselves in the harsh conditions?

2. Erro noticed that sunlight caused the huge crystals to grow out of the sand. Do any crystals form that quickly on Earth? Do some research and share what you find with your friends.

3. Zak and Erro work well together to escape their situation. But what would happen if they split up? Describe what you think each boy would need to do to survive in the desert on his own.

WRITE ABOUT IT

1. This story takes place on the Plateau of Leng. How do you think this area earned its name? Write a short story that explains how the Plateau of Leng got its name.

2. Erro is frightened of scorpion rats at first. But he later finds his courage and defeats one. Write about a time when you acted bravely in spite of being scared of something.

ABOUT THE AUTHOR

Michael Dahl is the author of more than 300 books for young readers, including the Library of Doom series. He is a huge fan of Star Trek, Star Wars and Doctor Who. He has a fear of closed-in spaces, but has visited several prisons, dungeons and strongholds, both ancient and modern. He made a daring escape from each one. Luckily, the guards still haven't found him.

ABOUT THE ILLUSTRATOR

Shen Fei loved comic books as a child. By the age of five he began making his own comic books and drew scenes from his favourite films. After graduating from art school he worked in the entertainment industry, creating art for films, games and books. Shen currently lives in Malaysia and works as a freelance illustrator for publishers all over the world. He also teaches at a local art school as a guest lecturer.

CONTENTS

ERRO

PLATEAU of LENG

PHANTOM FOREST

POISON SEA

VULCAN MOUNTAINS

LAKE of GOLD

METAL MOON

DIAMOND MINES

MONSTER ZOO

ITS OF NO RETURN

PRISON STRONGHOLDS

SWAMP OF FLAME

SCARLET JUNGLE

PRISON ENERGY DRIVES

SPACE PORT
RISONER INTAKE

ABYSS OF GIANTS

ZAK

THE PRISONERS

ZAK NINE

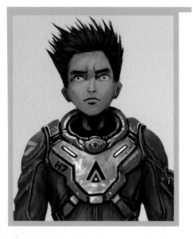

Zak is a teenage boy from Earth Base Zeta. He dreams of piloting a star fighter one day. Zak is very brave and is a quick thinker. But his enthusiasm often leads him into trouble.

ERRO

Erro is a teenage furling from the planet Quom. He has the fur, long tail, sharp eyes and claws of his species. Erro is often impatient with Zak's reckless ways. But he shares his friend's love of adventure.

THE PRISON PLANET

Alcatraz . . . there is no escape from this terrifying prison planet. It's filled with dungeons, traps, endless deserts and other dangers. Zak Nine and his alien friend, Erro, are trapped here. They had sneaked onto a ship hoping to see an awesome space battle. But the ship landed on Alcatraz instead. Now they have to work together if they ever hope to escape!

ZAK'S STORY . . . TRAPPED! >>>

Erro and I were recently caught in a canyon full of flesh-eating plants. Now the Alcatraz guards are taking us over a sickly-yellow sea to a new prison. They say this new place will teach us to obey the rules – but only if we can survive. . . .

>>>>

CHAPTER ONE:
CHAINED

Chains are the worst.

They're heavy. They dig into your wrists. And you can't unlock them without the key.

Erro and I are both chained to the deck of a hover ship.

We're prisoners on the ship with ten of the biggest, smelliest guards on Alcatraz.

When the hover ship slows to a stop, the guards undo our chains. I look out from the ship to see where we are. Yellowish clouds are boiling up from the sea below the ship.

Hovering over the sea are hundreds of metal cages. Each one swings on a chain hanging from a glowing sphere.

Each cage holds a single prisoner. Two empty cages sway near the hover ship . . . our new homes.

CHAPTER TWO:
BOTTOMLESS

The hover ship floats next to the empty cages.

"Get in!" grunts a guard, pointing with his laser spear.

I look closer at the metal cages. "They don't have a bottom," I say.

"How will we keep from falling out?" asks Erro.

"That's up to you," growls another, smellier guard. "But don't worry. The sea is poisonous acid. If you fall, your deaths will be quick – and *painful*."

My Quom friend and I each climb into an empty cage.

I grab the metal bars and brace my boots against the crossbars.

Below my bottomless cage,
the yellow sea boils and bubbles.
Sickly yellow mist rises up from the
surface. It doesn't smell very good.

I'm not sure how we'll get out of
this mess.

As the ship flies away, a guard yells, "If you're lucky, we might be back in two weeks."

"*Two weeks?*" I shout back. "How will we sleep? What will we eat?"

A guard laughs. "I think you mean, what will eat *you*!" the guard snorts. Then the ship is gone.

I don't like the guard's answer. What did he mean by that?

CHAPTER THREE:
JAWS

We've been here for two days. Erro is hanging below his cage, swinging from his tail.

"I hate closed-in spaces," he says. "At least we can get out of these things."

Suddenly a pair of giant, red eyes appears in the yellow acid below him. "Look out!" I shout.

A huge fish-thing leaps out of the poison sea. It opens its jaws towards Erro!

Erro screams. He jumps onto the dome of his cage.

KRRUNNNNCH!

The creature's huge jaws snap shut, and it falls back into the poison sea.

Erro turns his wide eyes to me. "Thank you for the warning," he says.

"You probably wouldn't taste that great anyway," I say. "Too much hair."

Erro is holding onto the chain at the top of his cage. "Not hair, fur," he says.

Erro looks at the glowing sphere holding up his cage.

"Touch it," I say.

"Why would I want to touch it?" asks Erro.

"To find out how it works," I reply.

"What if I accidentally turn it off?" he says. He looks down towards the yellow sea.

He's probably thinking of that giant fish-thing.

"That creature is gone," I say.

I know Erro doesn't believe me. But he reaches up towards the glowing ball.

"Whoa!" he shouts. He almost falls off his cage.

"What happened?" I ask.

"The sphere pushed away my arm," he says.

CHAPTER FOUR:
ESCAPE PLAN

"Try again. But do it harder this time," I say.

Erro reaches towards the sphere and tries to hit it. But his paw quickly bounces away from the glowing surface.

"It did it again!" he says.

The sphere is pushing stuff away,
I think. *It must be an anti-gravity field.*

That gives me an idea.

I start rocking my cage back and forth like a big swing. The other prisoners are laughing at me.

"What are you doing?" asks Erro.

"Rock yours too," I tell him. "Maybe we can connect our two cages."

"You have a plan," says Erro. "I am not going to like this, am I?"

"Hey, you can trust me," I say.

Erro starts rocking his cage too. Our cages start swinging closer and closer to each other. But not close enough.

"My tail!" shouts Erro. "Grab my tail."

When his cage swings close to me,
I reach through the bars and catch his
tail. I hope it doesn't hurt him.

"Pull!" he says.

I pull as hard as I can. Erro's cage draws closer and closer to mine.

When it's close enough, he reaches out and grabs my cage. Then I wrap my belt around the bars of both cages.

We're connected.

CHAPTER FIVE:
FLOATING TO FREEDOM

Erro wraps his belt around the bars too.

BOOOOMP!

We suddenly feel a sharp jolt.

"The cages are moving," says Erro.
"And we are not rocking them!"

When the scorpion moves closer,
Erro cups his hands around his mouth.
He tilts his head back and cries out.

SQQQQQUUUEEEEEEEEEE!

It is not a human sound.

Something rumbles high above. A large slab of crystal breaks off above our heads.

THOOOOM!!!

The broken slab of crystal falls and crushes the scorpion. Its deadly tail wriggles, and then it stops.

"Whoa! You broke that crystal with your voice," I say to Erro.

"It is a hunter's call from Quom," he says, smiling. "Sadly, it is not strong enough to open a passage through the crystal."

I step around the dead scorpion and stare down into the hole.

"That creepy-crawlie came from this hole," I say. "Maybe it can lead us out."

We crawl into the dark tunnel that travels deep under the ground.

"I hope there are no more scorpions," Erro says.

"Me too," I reply. Hopefully the tunnel will lead us somewhere safe. . . .

GLOSSARY

crystal mineral or rock with a regular pattern of many flat surfaces

device tool that does a particular job

dungeon prison, usually underground

meteor piece of rock that falls from space

passage corridor or tunnel

plateau area of high, flat land

reflect return light from the surface of an object

scorpion animal related to a spider with pincers and a jointed tail tipped with a poisonous stinger

skitter move in a quick or jerky way

species group of living things that share similar features

trail follow the tracks or signs left behind by animals, people or moving objects